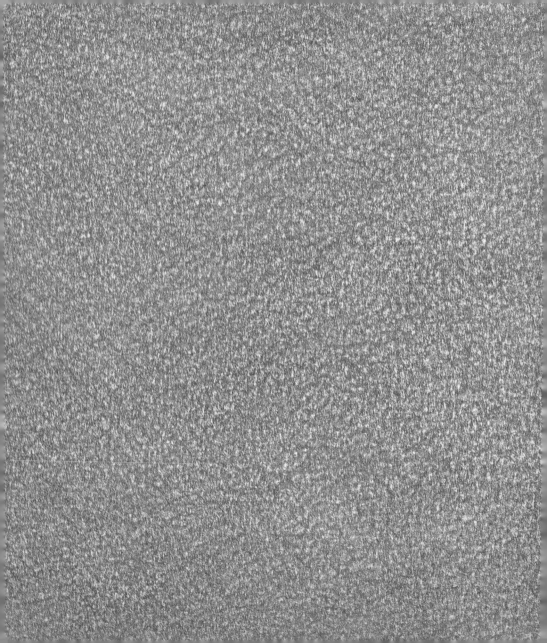

First published 1994 by Walker Books Ltd
87 Vauxhall Walk, London SE11 5HJ

This edition produced 1999 for
The Book People Ltd, Hall Wood Avenue
Haydock, St Helens WA11 9UL

Printed in Hong Kong

ISBN 0-7445-2670-1

My Big Machine

Written by Richard James
Illustrated by Chris Winn

TED SMART

Today I'm an inventor,

I'm making
a big machine –

out of bottles and
cardboard boxes

and paper
and Plasticine

and bits of
a broken umbrella,

and some string and
the lids of some jars –

and later tonight, when the
moon's big and bright,

I'll fly my machine
to the stars.

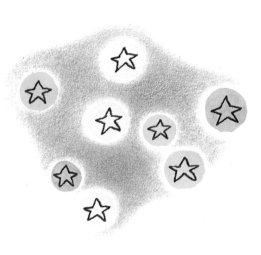